D1081170

d

THIS BOOK BELONGS TO:

. . . .

'FOR GRACE' - E.L.
'FOR MY MUM, JOAN' - L.P.

OXFORD
UNIVERSITY PRESS

Great Clarendon Street, Oxford OX2 6DP

Oxford University Press is a department of the University of Oxford.
It furthers the University's objective of excellence in research, scholarship,
and education by publishing worldwide. Oxford is a registered trade mark of
Oxford University Press in the UK and in certain other countries

First published 2004
This edition first published 2019

British Library Cataloguing in Publication Data
Data available

ISBN: 978-0-19-276887-2

1 3 5 7 9 10 8 6 4 2

Printed in China

Paper used in the production of this book is a natural,
recyclable product made from wood grown in sustainable forests.
The manufacturing process conforms to the environmental
regulations of the country of origin.

BEAUTIFUL BANANAS

ELIZABETH LAIRD

ILLUSTRATED BY LIZ PICHON

OXFORD

UNIVERSITY PRESS

'Goodbye, Mama,' says Beatrice. She's on her way to see her grandad. She's got a present for him. It's a beautiful bunch of bananas.

On the way, she meets a giraffe, who flicks his tufty tail. He whisks the bananas right off Beatrice's head and they land with a splash in the stream.

'Oh, I'm sorry,' says the giraffe. He picks some flowers, and bends down low, and gives the bunch to Beatrice. 'My grandad will like these,' she says.

A swarm of bees settles on the
flowers. 'Hey!' Beatrice cries.
She beats the bees off, but the
flowers are crushed and spoiled.

'We're very sorry,' say the bees. They wrap up some honeycomb, and give it to Beatrice instead. On she goes, down the path.

Some naughty monkeys see the honeycomb. 'We like honey!' they cry. They snatch it away from Beatrice. All the honey drips on to the ground.

'Stop!' says Beatrice. 'That honey was for my grandad.' 'Oh dear,' say the monkeys. They run up into the trees and pick some mangoes for her instead.

Beatrice takes
the mangoes
and hurries on.

Suddenly, out jumps a lion! 'Aaghh!' screams Beatrice. She's very, very scared. She drops the mangoes, and they all roll away.

'It's all right,' says the lion. 'I didn't mean to frighten you.' He pulls out one of his whiskers and gives it to her. Beatrice runs on, holding the whisker in her hand.

A parrot sees the whisker. He thinks it's a twig. He swoops down, and carries it off to build his nest. 'Come back!' shouts Beatrice. 'That whisker's for my grandad!'

'My mistake,' squawks the parrot. He pulls a long feather out of his tail, and gives it to Beatrice. On she goes again.

But what's that long grey thing, dangling down beside the path? Beatrice doesn't see it. Accidentally, she brushes it with her feather.

'You're ti-ti-tickling me!' gasps the elephant.
'Atishoo!' His sneeze blows the feather away.

The elephant is sorry. He stretches out his
trunk, and picks a bunch of bananas. Beatrice
claps her hands. 'Oh, thank you,' she says.
'Bananas are best, after all.'

Here at last is Grandad's house, and here at last is Grandad. 'I've got something for you,' says Beatrice, and she gives him the bananas.

IDEAS FOR WHEN YOU'RE SHARING BEAUTIFUL BANANAS

- What colour are bananas? What other fruits and vegetables can you think of that are the same colour as bananas? Look out for other things that are the same colour as bananas as you share the story.

- Lots of tiny birds, bugs, and beasties appear on the pages of this book. Try pointing at each one you spot while you listen to the story!

- Bananas are tasty and also very good for you. Can you think of some delicious things that are made with bananas? What is your favourite way to eat a banana?

- When you listen to the story, keep an eye out for those bananas. Every time you see a bunch of bananas you could shout out: 'bananas!'

- In this story have you spotted that sometimes a little pair of eyes looks out at you from the leaves? Who do you think they might belong to? You could draw the eyes in the middle of a sheet of paper and then draw your creature around them!

- Jungles can be noisy places! Can you munch like a giraffe, buzz like a bee, 'ooo-ooo' like a monkey, roar like a lion, squawk like a parrot, sneeze like an elephant . . . and chuckle like a grandad?

- Words can often sound fun to read aloud, just like: 'a bunch of beautiful bananas'. Can you suggest some words to describe the other fruits and treats that appear in this story? Think about the sound and rhythm of the words you choose. How would you describe . . . a pineapple? Some mangoes? Flowers? Honey?

- Can you find the page where the monkeys are in the mango tree? How many mangoes can you count on the tree? And how many mangoes can you count that are not on the tree?

- At the end of this story Beatrice arrives at her Grandad's house and lots of the friendly animals that she met along the way are there, too. What do you think happens on Beatrice's journey back home?